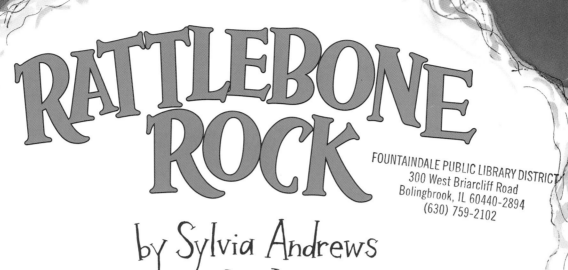

RATTLEBONE ROCK

by Sylvia Andrews

illustrated by Jennifer Plecas

HarperCollins Publishers

Rattlebone Rock
Text copyright © 1995 by Sylvia Andrews
Illustrations copyright © 1995 by Jennifer Plecas
Printed in Mexico. All rights reserved.

Library of Congress Cataloging-in-Publication Data
Andrews, Sylvia.
    Rattlebone Rock / by Sylvia Andrews ; pictures by
Jennifer Plecas.
        p.   cm.
    Summary: When skeletons, ghouls, witches, and assorted
other spooky creatures take up the rock beat, a town has its
best-ever Halloween.
    ISBN 0-06-023451-2. — ISBN 0-06-023452-0 (lib. bdg.)
ISBN 0-06-443484-2 (pbk.)
Jennifer, ill.   II. Title.
PZ8.3.A5489Rat   1995   93-4426
[E]—dc20   CIP
                                                    AC

            First Harper Trophy edition 1997.

For David and Kent
—S.A.

For Andrea and Stephanie
—J.P.

Folks in the town
Still talk of the night
When the moon on the graveyard
Shone so bright
That the spirits there
Made the tombstones knock
And the beat began
For the Rattlebone Rock.

BOOMA-BOOM! BOOMA-BOOM!

Skeletons danced
And pranced around.
They rattled their bones
With a rhythmic sound.

Ghosts swayed in line
To the beat of the bones
And jazzed up the sound
With musical moans.

Ghouls jumped right in
With a rapping rhyme
And tapped on tombs
To the BOOMA-BOOM time!

Then a banshee rose
And began to wail
Like the shriek of wind
In a rollicking gale.

And grizzly goblins
Howled and hissed
As they shuffle-shoe danced
In the syncopating mist.

Weird witches, too,
Stirred a simmering brew
And chanted spells
While the BOOM beat grew.

The beat was heard
All through the town
As windows shook
And pots fell down.

Then cradles swayed

ROCKA-ROCK!

ROCKA-ROCK!

And clocks ran wild

TICKA-TOCK!
TICKA-TOCK!

Everyone rushed
Outside to see
What was making the town
Shake crazily.

The townsfolk cheered
When they saw the scene.
It looked like
The best-ever Halloween.
So they all joined in
And stomped their feet!
Even the mayor
Boogied to the beat.

Bats swooped in the sky

SQUEAKA-SQUEAK!   SQUEAKA-SQUEAK!

Cats made a din

MEEEA-OOO! MEEEA-OOO!

That BOOMA-BOOM beat
Kept on and on
So everyone rocked
Till the light of dawn.

Now folks still talk
Of that wild, wild night
When the moon on the graveyard
Shone so bright
That the spirits there
Made the tombstones knock
And the whole town danced
To the Rattlebone Rock.